Tusk

To Sheldon,

Lyle Nee

Also by Lyle Weis:

No Problem, We'll Fix It

The Mill Under His Skin

Burn It

Bush Party

Let's Wrestle

TUSK

Lyle Weis

iUniverse, Inc.
New York Lincoln Shanghai

TUSK

iUniverse books may be ordered through booksellers or by contacting:

iUniverse
2021 Pine Lake Road, Suite 100
Lincoln, NE 68512
www.iuniverse.com
1-800-Authors (1-800-288-4677)

Because of the dynamic nature of the Internet, any Web addresses or links contained in this book may have changed since publication and may no longer be valid.

This is a work of fiction. All of the characters, names, incidents, organizations, and dialogue in this novel are either the products of the author's imagination or are used fictitiously.

ISBN: 978-0-595-47855-2

Printed in the United States of America

Acknowledgements

A huge thank you to Dar Renner, for her patient reading of the manuscript, general encouragement and insight.

My gratitude to Jena Snyder, for her expert editorial advice.

And thanks to Christina Grant, Alicia Karl and Austin Johncox for their insightful readings and comments.

Finally, I wish to acknowledge artist Robert Woodbury for the skill and interpretation he brings to the illustrations for this book.

Prologue

The boar stood thirty nine inches at the shoulder and weighed just over 1000 pounds. His body was almost three feet wide and covered by short, dark hairs. Powerful and smart, he could run as fast as a bear. Since breaking out of his pen, the boar had roamed the little island looking for food. This afternoon he was in the garden, rooting around for carrots. Soon his farmer would find and pen him up again.

Suddenly he stopped digging in the dirt and listened. Something was crossing the wooden bridge that spanned the water to the cabin. The boar stared at the gate, waiting. A fox poked its head past the steel grating and climbed through to the dirt driveway. It came his way, moving oddly from side to side.

The boar stared as the fox came closer. There was something wrong with the little animal, the way it staggered. The boar tensed his leg muscles, ready to attack. The fox came very near to him, only to stumble and fall over. Curious, the boar nudged it with one of his six-inch tusks.

The fox uncoiled like a spring, snarling, and sank its fangs into the boar's snout.

Howling in pain, the boar raised his head and swung the fox like a hooked fish through the air. He slammed it to the ground and drove a tusk cleanly through the fox's body into the dirt. Raising his head and the impaled animal, the boar gave a powerful twist of his neck. The fox's lifeless body flew from the tusk across the garden and hit a tree.

The boar blinked and huffed, waiting for the fox to attack again. When it did not, he turned toward the river. Already the pain from the puncture wounds in his snout was fading. In a day he would not remember the fox.

But as the boar drank from the fresh water, the rabies virus was already riding the blood trail through his body.

1

Two Weeks Later

Nick Thorsby finished his breakfast, a piece of toast and coffee. Movement by the easy chair caught his eye. A mouse poked its nose into the air, sniffing, hoping for some crumbs.

"Get lost!" Nick tramped his foot on the wooden floor, and the mouse disappeared. The little critters were getting awfully bold. But, the truth be told, Nick didn't mind them that much, except for the mess. He had lived alone for most of his seventy years and the mice were company. Nick figured you couldn't be fussy about some things.

"Here you go." Nick tossed a tiny corner of toast across the floor. It disappeared under the chair. "Last piece."

He stood and looked at the kitchen. That wasn't just the last piece of toast. The large water jug was empty, and so were most of the cupboards. It was high time to make a trip into town for supplies. He was out of food, soap and a lot of other things.

"Guess I better feed that hog before I leave," he said aloud, though there was nobody but the mouse to hear him in the little cabin. He opened the door and slipped into a pair of rubber boots.

Nick raised a few pigs and sometimes bred them with wild boars. In the fall he had sold or slaughtered the rest of the pigs. Once he had the money, he would start to rebuild the stock. Now he had only one animal left, a boar he had bought a few weeks before. A huge creature. The big one was special and he was worried about it. The past few days it had been behaving oddly. He hoped it wasn't sick.

Nick drew out his key ring and locked the deadbolt on the cabin. Then he crossed the yard to the corral beside the rundown barn, twirling his keys on his finger as he walked. Usually the boar heard him coming and squealed, knowing it was time to eat. This time, there was no sound. The farmer unlatched the gate and stepped inside the pen. At first, he didn't see the boar.

"Not again." Nick shook his head. "Now where did you get out this time?"

He began to walk around the pen, looking for a telltale broken board. Then he heard a sound by the water trough. He turned to see the boar struggle to its feet. The animal was caked with mud and the long tusks at the sides of its mouth were filthy.

Nick took two steps toward the boar then stopped. He saw the long strings of saliva hanging from the mouth, the wild eyes, and knew.

"Aw no," Nick said. His keys fell from his hand as he turned to flee.

He almost made it to the gate before the boar caught him.

2

Late that same afternoon, a kilometer away

Jordan twisted the throttle on his father's quad. The Honda engine revved and coughed, sending puffs of black exhaust smoke into the forest air. He frowned and turned the key so that the engine stopped. Then he spoke to the girl standing beside him.

"Sounds like the air cleaner is dirty, or there's some grit in the fuel line." He grinned teasingly. "This will just take a second, Amanda. How about you buy us something cold to drink?"

Amanda looked out at the little valley ahead. After school, she and Jordan had decided to go for a ride. They were on a forestry service road, a rough and narrow path that stretched up and down again through the wilderness about twenty minutes from their hometown of Bear Hill, Alberta. There wasn't a building in sight. As far as she could see there were trees, hills, and in the distance, mountains.

"Sure, I'll duck into the nearest store," she joked. "Be back before you know it."

"That's my girl. Talented, too." Jordan tilted up the rear seat. Underneath was the engine and he unscrewed the air cleaner.

Amanda glanced at the position of the sun, already low in the sky. "We should get back. Aren't you hungry?"

He removed the filter and inspected it. "Well, everything looks okay."

Lowering the seat, he pointed down the cleared pathway. "We're almost at Thorsby's place. It's like, just over the next hill."

Amanda frowned. Jordan was always stretching stuff out. One more hill, one more game, one more drink. She loved him, but he had trouble stopping … anything. They had arguments about that, especially his drinking.

"Tell me again why we're going there?"

"He raises pigs on this little island in the middle of the river. He's, like, a hermit." Jordan made a circling motion with his finger, beside his head. "A little crazy, but he wouldn't hurt anybody."

She put her hands on her hips. "And I would want to meet him because … why, exactly?"

"Well, I just want to talk to him." His face broke into a smile. "He said he has a new pig, a giant."

Amanda didn't like the way Jordan avoided giving a direct answer. A doubt came to her. "You're not buying something from him, are you?"

Lately Jordan had started hanging around with Ryan, a guy their age from town. Everybody knew Ryan was heavy into alcohol and other stuff. Amanda wondered if they were buying drugs from someone. Maybe this hermit farmer.

Jordan frowned. "Aw, come on, Amanda. You're not going to give me a big sermon, are you?"

She didn't want to get into an argument. They fought too often about the drinking anyway. She looked out at the trees, all the trees. A sudden uneasy thought came to her.

"Jordan?"

"Yeah."

"You think there are bears around here?"

"Haven't see one."

"Okay, but that doesn't mean there aren't any."

"If you're worried, Amanda, just make some noise. That'll keep them away."

Noise. Well, that wasn't a problem when the quad was running. It was plenty noisy. But not now. "What kind of noise?"

"Sing. That'll scare anything."

She picked up a branch and threw it at him. It bounced off his back.

"Hey, careful, you'll kill the mechanic. Then you'll be sorry."

She leaned back to rest on the wild grass. The sky was a beautiful blue, with some large fluffy clouds drifting over the hill. A perfect afternoon. If you didn't think about bears.

She listened to him working for a while, then remembered something. "Did your dad get that job at the sawmill?"

Jordan didn't answer at first. "No."

"So, is he going to try to get work in High Prairie?"

Jordan took a deep breath. "There's a problem."

She thought he meant with the engine. "Can't fix it? So, I guess we're walking."

"I don't mean that." He lowered the engine cover again. "Dad's talking about moving to Edmonton."

"What?" She sat up. Edmonton was almost four hours away. When?"

"Next month."

Jordan lived alone with his dad. If his dad moved, then....

"Are you going with him?"

He shook his head. "I dunno. Guess so."

"What about us?"

"We could see each other on weekends." He stared miserably at the ground. "And use email to keep in touch, or phone."

She had an idea, though not a great one. "Is there any chance you could stay in town, with your aunt and uncle?" Jordan's aunt Teena was a wonderful person, even though his uncle wasn't.

Jordan made a face. "I don't think so. They're having troubles. Their place is not real peaceful now."

She wasn't surprised. Jordan's uncle drank way too much, and when he did there were bad arguments. Sometimes Jordan's aunt had bruises on her face and arms. Once his uncle had stood outside, weaving back and forth, firing a shotgun into the air. People in town were afraid of him.

There was an awkward silence.

"Why didn't you tell me?"

"I wanted to, but couldn't find the right time."

"Oh, great!" She felt hot tears welling up. "This is stupid."

"Yeah." He turned back to the quad.

She blinked and wiped her face with a sleeve. She hated Jordan's dad then, and his job, and Edmonton. She even hated the sky and the stupid trees.

The engine coughed, sputtered, then roared to life. Jordan got onto the seat. "Uh ... are you still okay to do this?"

A part of her wanted to turn around and head back to town. But now she realized this might be one of their last rides together, for a long time.

"Okay," she said. "But no more detours. Promise?"

Jordan placed a hand over his heart. "Promise."

Jordan gave her a delighted smile over his shoulder and the quad jerked forward. She wrapped her arms tightly around his chest as the machine bounced along the forestry service road.

3

The quad climbed another hill, then swept down the opposite slope. Over Jordan's shoulder, Amanda saw a clearing ahead where the sun twinkled on water and pointed ahead.

"Glacier River," he shouted. "We're almost there."

He slowed the machine. Spring rains had cut little streams across the trail in places, and some of the ruts were deep. The quad bounced and Amanda dug her fingers into Jordan's chest. He turned his face in a grimace. "Ouch!"

Serves you right, she thought. Dragging me out here for a bone rattling ride like this.

Suddenly the trail sloped down into a clearing. Ahead was a river that split in two to flow around an island. On the island was a small cabin, with a barn. A large open space that looked like it might be a garden separated the two buildings.

The dirt road in front of Amanda and Jordan ran up to a bridge that spanned the river. A steel gate blocked the way on the other side of the bridge. She wondered what kind of person would live there, alone, surrounded by water?

Jordan drove down the road to the edge of the bridge and stopped. He shifted the quad into neutral and spoke above the noise of the engine. "What do you think? Isn't it great?"

The trail crossed the bridge and ended in front of the hermit's place. The cabin was made of split logs with a door and one window at the front.

The steel gate had a sign: KEEP OUT. "This guy must like his privacy," Amanda said.

"The sign? Don't worry, he never locks it."

Jordan walked over to the gate, flipped the latch, and pushed it open.

"Should you being doing that?" She looked nervously toward the cabin.

Jordan came back to the machine. "It's okay, but he likes to keep it closed. The pigs could get out."

Jordan revved the motor and they started to cross.

The bridge was narrow, just wide enough for a vehicle. As they slowly drove over, Amanda had a good view of the fast, muddy water of the river below. It churned and slapped at the old bridge. She tried to ignore a broken board on her side.

Amanda had always been nervous around water. When she was little her older sister and brother took her down to the river near their house. They played on the bank until she slipped and fell in. When they pulled her out she was unconscious. She had woken up later on the ground, choking and coughing.

To her relief, the quad made it to the other side and pulled up a few paces from the cabin. Jordan dismounted and ran back to close the gate. Then he strode to the cabin door and knocked.

Amada studied the cabin. The board sides, never painted, had faded to grey. A metal stove chimney leaned over like a rusty finger and weeds grew all around, partly hiding some broken wooden crates and garden tools. An old kitchen chair was propped against the cabin. The door was closed, and tattered grey curtains covered the one front window.

Jordan tried the door handle. To Amanda's relief, it didn't open. He walked to the side of the cabin and disappeared from view. Sometimes he just ignored her, doing whatever seemed to pop into his head. Like now. Irritated, she followed him.

"What are you up to?" she asked.

"I want to see if he's around back," he said. "Come on."

The ground was uneven, with thistles growing thickly. At the back of the cabin there was a single cracked window that looked out at the woods and steep cliffs across the river. She spotted a small wooden shack about twenty paces into the trees.

"All the comforts of home," she said. The outhouse door hung open and a one-hole bench was in plain view.

"Need to take a break?" Jordan snickered.

"I can wait."

Jordan called out. "Nick?"

His voice rose to die out among the trees. Amanda crossed her arms. The sooner they left, the better. The farm was creepy. "Can we go now?"

"Just a sec. Maybe he's in the barn."

Jordan led the way toward the sad-looking structure with a sagging roof. Amanda was beginning to feel uneasy and she scanned their surroundings. To their left was a large neglected garden that stretched up from the river and ended at the dirt driveway. In the middle of the clearing stood a scarecrow, complete with a faded blue baseball cap, white tattered shirt and blue coveralls. Down by the river raspberry canes grew wild.

The main door of the barn was ajar and Jordan stepped inside. "Nick?"

Amanda stood at the doorway. Her nostrils caught a heavy odor of rotting hay mixed with manure. She saw a small tractor parked in the shadows and boxes and tools stacked against a wall. It was very quiet in the darkened space.

"He might be over at the pig pen." Jordan left the barn and walked around toward the pen. As Amanda followed him, she saw a light blue pickup parked a short distance away.

"Someone is sitting in the truck," she said. A grey-haired man was visible through the side window.

"Hey, that's him," Jordan said. He called out. "Nick!"

There was no answer. "He's a little hard of hearing sometimes." Jordan called again.

The figure in the truck didn't move and Jordan reached down to grab Amanda's hand. "Come on, I'll introduce you."

They reached the side of the pickup and Amanda felt a chill sweep over her. "There's something wrong with him," she said in a low voice.

4

Nick Thorsby was in the driver's seat, slumped forward. His mouth hung open slightly.

"He's probably fallen asleep. Watch him jump." Jordan grabbed the door handle and pulled.

As the door opened, Nick toppled outward. Jordan tried to catch him, but the old man slipped away and fell to the ground.

Amanda gasped and grabbed Jordan's arm. Nick's clothing was coated in blood. His shirt had slid up and a gash stretched over his belly with a lot of dried blood smeared across his skin.

Trembling, Amanda turned from the ghastly sight and buried her face against Jordan's chest. She could feel his heart pounding. "What should we do?" she managed to ask.

"We need to get help for him."

With shaking hands she took out her cell phone and flipped open the cover. A message appeared on the display: *No Signal Available.*

"We're out of range," Amanda said. They were a long way, she realized, from help.

"He's not …," Jordan began. He leaned forward but didn't let go of her. "I don't think he's breathing."

She forced herself to peek again at the man's body. "Do you think he's …?"

In a whisper, Jordan said, "I don't know. Stay back."

He kneeled down and touched the man's cheek. "His skin is cold." He stood again and backed up a couple of steps. "I think he's dead."

Amanda stared at the man, stunned. She saw now that he had cuts on his hands and face. Her eyes were unable to avoid the gaping wound to his stomach. "What … what happened to him?"

Jordan stood quickly and put his arm around her. She felt his body shaking.

"I don't know," he said. "Maybe he was using a saw or something."

She fought the wave of nausea swirling upwards in her throat. For a moment, they could only stand and stare at the body.

Jordan shook his head. "It looks like he tried to drive for help but bled to death."

Suddenly Amanda could feel her horror slipping into something else: fear. The wounds on Nick's body looked more like an attack than an accident.

"What if," she whispered, "a bear did this?" She looked anxiously at the garden, the barn and the woods beyond. "We have to get out of here."

Jordan stood like a statue. His eyes seemed unable to pull away from Nick.

"Please, let's go!" Amanda jerked Jordan away and they ran toward the quad. He straddled the machine and pressed the start button. The electric starter motor whirred but the engine didn't start.

"Aw, come on!" Jordan pounded the steering bar.

He coaxed the starter again, with no luck. Then suddenly the engine coughed and roared to life. Jordan revved it several times, but the engine choked and sputtered before it died again.

◆   ◆   ◆

Just beyond Amanda's sight, the boar stood in a cluster of aspen trees. It had wandered out of the pen after attacking the farmer. Sick and confused, the boar had stumbled to the trees and fallen asleep. Until the noise woke him.

A roaring from near the cabin hurt the boar's ears and made his head feel ready to explode. The animal tried to swallow, only to discover sharp pain. Water would soothe the rawness. But the urge to drink from the river brought fear and pain. The boar whined. A thousand little fires burned in his throat.

When the boar stood, his legs were stiff and he trembled. Over by the cabin was the quad. To the boar, the machine looked like another big animal, with two humans beside it. The machine roared, coughed, became silent. Then it roared again. One of the humans climbed on its back while the other stood nearby.

The big animal was still now, but the boar could hear Jordan and Amanda talking and their words were a cackle, a horrible aching sound in his brain. The boar grunted, lowered his head and pushed through the bushes. He needed to stop the noise.

◆　　◆　　◆

Amanda saw movement about a hundred feet away in the trees. Instantly, she forgot about the quad and Nick. An animal walked out of the forest and stood in the clearing near the old garden. It wasn't a deer or a wolf. And it didn't seem to be a bear.

"Jordan."

"Yeah."

"Something's over there."

Jordan turned and they watched as the creature walked into the garden and stopped. Amanda had never seen anything like it.

"Is that a pig?"

Jordan stared. "Nick said he had a wild boar. Kind of a monster pig."

The animal stood still. From where they were, it looked bigger than the quad. It was dark brown, with a rough hide. And there was something else.

Amanda stared. "What's that in its face?" The pig or hog or whatever had chunks of wood or something sticking up from its lower jaw.

Jordan's voice dropped to a near-whisper. "Those are ... tusks."

Now Amanda remembered. Their science teacher had brought some newspaper clippings into class, including a picture of a huge, scary-looking pig called a boar. It had nasty-looking tusks that the teacher said could rip a person open, no problem. The animal on the road now looked even bigger and these tusks stuck out further.

"It's acting weird," Jordan said.

The boar hadn't moved, but its body was weaving. As they watched it teetered sideways and almost fell.

"It's sick." Amanda moved closer to Jordan. "I don't like this."

The boar raised its head and stared in their direction as if it had seen them for the first time. It swayed from side to side and staggered like a drunk. Then it began to zigzag toward the quad.

"Hurry." Amanda scrambled onto the back seat just as the boar began to trot. No mistake, it was coming for them.

Frantically Jordan twisted the ignition key. As the boar came closer, Amanda saw that it drooled. Long ropes of saliva hung from its mouth and trailed to the ground. She could hear the animal's breathing, heavy and ragged.

The quad starter ground away, but the engine didn't start. "Come on," Jordan pleaded.

The boar broke into a run as it lowered its head and charged.

5

The animal raced across the clearing. It was faster than a human, probably as fast as a moose. Before Amanda or Jordan could react, the boar slammed into the quad, hitting the left front tire. The machine bucked and suddenly the two teens were airborne. Amanda landed a short distance away on her back. Jordan fell near the quad. Dazed, he rose from his hands and knees. The boar stood only a few feet away, watching. Then the animal lunged.

Swinging its head, the boar slashed Jordan's leg. He screamed and fell over onto the quad. His attacker backed up and hammered the side of the machine again, shaking Jordan like a rag doll.

The boar paused, watching Jordan. Then, swaying and breathing heavily, it stumbled across the garden and disappeared into the trees.

Amanda got up and ran to the quad. Jordan was conscious but his face was ashen. He moaned.

"I'm here," Amanda said.

Jordan clenched his teeth together. His pant leg was ripped open, revealing a gash. Blood ran from the wound.

Amanda knew the injury was bad. "We need to wrap that."

Jordan nodded and sat up. "First aid kit is in … the storage bin under the seat."

Amanda lifted the seat and found a red box with a white cross on top. She flipped open the kit and her heart sank. Inside were a few small bandages, a roll of white tape and gauze. The cut on Jordan's leg was longer than her hand.

"I'll get you taped up, then we need to get out of here."

She grabbed the sides of his ripped pant leg and began to pull them apart. Jordan winced.

"Sorry." Her hands were shaking.

Taking a deep breath, she packed gauze against the gash and twisted white tape around his thigh to hold it in place. Blood immediately seeped through the bandage.

"We need help." Jordan looked away from his leg.

Amanda reached into a pocket. Maybe her cell phone would work now. When she turned it over to dial, she gasped. The phone was cracked across the display. Sure enough, when she pressed the power button, nothing happened.

"My phone's broken."

Jordan closed his eyes. "You'll have to drive us out."

She looked at the quad and shook her head.

"Even if I could start it, we wouldn't get far. The tire is ruined."

The pain made Jordan wince. "What … what about Nick's truck?"

She looked longingly at the blue pickup. Then her eyes nervously checked the barn, the garden, the trees beyond. So many places for the beast to wait, to hide. And Jordan had trouble walking, let alone running.

"I don't want to take the chance. The boar would cut us off."

Their eyes met and then they both looked in the direction of the bridge. If they could put the gate between themselves and the boar….

Amanda knew there was no other choice. "Can you walk?"

"Maybe. Give me a hand."

He swung his good leg over the side of the vehicle. She helped him lift the injured one and he slid to the ground.

"How does it feel?"

"Not great." Jordan's face was pale. "Let's get started."

She draped his arm over her shoulder. They took only a few steps toward the bridge before he stopped.

"Just a sec," he said. He paused, took a deep breath. "This might take a while."

"Okay." She eyed the trees nervously. "If we can just make it past the gate."

His eyes widened at something behind her and she spun around to follow his gaze. The boar had come out of the woods again, swinging its head from side to side. It was coming their way.

The bridge was too far.

"Hurry," Amanda urged. "Let's take cover behind the quad."

Quickly, with Jordan hopping on one leg, they made it back to the wrecked machine and ducked behind it. The boar didn't seem to notice them, heading instead for the front of the cabin.

"We can't stay here," Amanda said. "If it comes over and sees us...."

Jordan took a deep breath and held his leg. Blood had soaked through the bandage and when he took his hand away his fingers were stained red. Amanda wondered how much time they had.

"I need to get you cleaned up and wrap the wound better. If only we could get inside the cabin."

"C—can't." Jordan gasped. "It's locked."

She nodded. "Let's go around the back of the cabin. We need a place to hide."

She helped him up and they hurried, like a couple in a three-legged race, around the side of the cabin.

Jordan leaned against the wall and slid down to sit. "My leg really hurts."

Amanda checked the back of the cabin. There was no back door, just the window about shoulder height off the ground. She reached up and pushed against the frame, with no luck. "It's latched."

"Break it."

"Too much noise. The sound might bring the boar here before we got inside."

The window looked as if it was made to open outward. She tried to pry her fingers under the edge and it moved a little.

"If we had a knife or something, I could slip it under the frame and push the latch aside."

Jordan took a deep breath. "In the tool kit under the seat there's a screwdriver."

"I'll get it, but I don't want to leave you here alone. If the pig comes this way...." She nervously peeked around the corner of the cabin.

"Jordan, can you walk a bit further?"

"I think so."

"I want you to hide in there." She pointed to the outhouse.

"What? You must be kidding. Nope, not in there."

"Would you rather take a chance on the pig?"

He hung his head. "Help me up, okay?"

She helped him to his feet, and they shuffled over to the outhouse. A powerful stench hit their noses. Amanda held her breath, and stepped inside. Then she helped Jordan in, and he slumped to the wooden floor.

"Hurry." He grabbed the rope handle on the inside of the door and held it partly shut.

"Okay," Amanda whispered.

6

Taking a deep breath, she sprinted to the quad. She lifted the storage lid and saw a grey metal toolbox. Opening it, she found the screwdriver. Amanda ran to the back of the cabin and flattened herself against the wall under the window.

"Jordan," she said in a loud whisper.

The door of the outhouse opened a crack. "Yeah?"

"Got it."

"Good. Let me help." The door began to open.

"No. You can barely walk. I'll do it."

She inserted the blade under the window frame and wiggled it. There was a sound of metal clicking on metal. Amanda pushed to the right. No luck. She took the blade out and tried again, this time pushing to the left. Through the glass she saw the latch handle move. With another push, the handle disappeared from view and the window itself popped out a tiny bit.

Amanda pried until the window gapped open. She raised it and peered inside.

An old smell, sweat mixed with mildew and something else heavy and unhealthy, escaped past her face. She caught a glimpse of a bed and a table and chairs. A sofa or large chair was beside the door. The countertop was covered with clutter: dirty plates, an empty tuna tin and several beer cans. It wasn't a pretty place, but then they weren't looking for a home. Just a safe hideout. She had to get inside.

Amanda hauled herself up. Half way in, with her legs dangling outside, she felt something brush up against her foot.

"Jordan, what are you doing?"

She looked back, and froze.

The pig was right below her. Its face was dirty and one side of its snout was swollen and raw. The boar's mouth hung open, and thick mucous dripped from its lip onto the ground. Two little black eyes stared at her.

Worst of all were the tusks. They looked almost as long as her forearm, and the left one was crooked and curved upward. It was smeared red, thick and dark. *Blood*, she realized with a shudder. Nick's, and now Jordan's, blood.

Amanda frantically pulled herself forward just as the boar slammed into the cabin wall. She fell forward and landed inside. There was a loud snort and the cabin shook again. The window banged shut and a piece of glass crashed to the floor.

Then everything was silent.

She scrambled to her feet and lifted the window. The boar had backed up and now stared at her. It huffed and wheeled around. Sniffing the ground, it began to walk toward the outhouse.

She screamed. "Jordan! Look out. It's coming!"

The pig stopped to look back at her. It seemed to be thinking. She used to believe that pigs were stupid, but those eyes seemed full of thoughts. Evil thoughts.

The boar lowered its head. It sniffed again before turning to stare at the outhouse.

"Oh no," she whispered. She could picture the beast smashing that fragile little structure to bits. Trampling Jordan.

Nose to the worn path, the boar set its hooves in a line to the outhouse. It pushed its snout against the crack of the door. Amanda watched, horrified: *It's trying to open the door!*

Amanda looked behind her for something, anything, to distract the boar. She spotted a can of beans beside the sink. Grabbing it, she scrambled to the window.

"Hey you! Hey, pig!"

She reached out the window and threw the can, hitting the pig on its hip. With an irritated squeal, the animal jerked around to look at the can. The boar swung its head at the object and suddenly the can was airborne, flying away to land with a clatter in the trees. The distraction had worked. Seeming to forget Amanda and Jordan, the boar trotted off around the corner of the cabin.

Amanda waited and listened.

"Jordan!" She tried to be as quiet as possible, but even a whisper seemed to break through the afternoon silence. No answer.

A new fear made her heart pound. What if he had passed out, alone in that awful place? "Please, Jordan, can you hear me?"

When he didn't reply, Amanda went to the front door of the cabin. Opening it a crack, she saw the boar wandering away. She slipped outside, sprinted around the cabin to the outhouse and yanked open the door.

Jordan had slumped to his side on the floor. She fell to her knees and put her face next to his. "Jordan! Can you hear me?"

He was unconscious, but breathing. His face was slick with sweat. An eyelid fluttered open.

"Wh-what happened?"

She was so relieved to see him conscious. "I think you blacked out. You have to get out of here."

"Uh. Okay."

She helped him sit up. The inside of the little toilet was hot and stank horribly.

"Can you stand?"

"Maybe."

His face was pale, his eyes bloodshot. When she tried to pull him up he winced. "Can you make it to the cabin door?"

"I … I don't know."

She helped him to his feet. He felt heavy and for a moment she thought he would collapse. But, shuffling like an old man, he began to walk. Amanda put his arm over her shoulder and together they slowly made their way to the side of the cabin. Before they got to the front, a roar erupted from the garden.

The boar was there, staring down the scarecrow. A breeze fluttered the sleeve of the scarecrow and the boar skittered backwards, huffing at the movement. Then it lowered its head and attacked. The scarecrow's wooden frame cracked and the cloth head went flying. Wood splinters and clothing scattered in all directions.

Abruptly the animal stopped its rampage to walk through the garden and down the slope toward the river. It staggered and cried out as if in pain.

Jordan raised his head. "Where is it?"

"Wandering near the river. He's in another world, out of his mind."

"Good. Maybe he's going to die."

"Come on. Let's get inside."

They managed only a few steps when the air was pierced by a shriek. The boar had gone to the water's edge and stumbled into it. Water flew as the beast churned out of the river and up the bank.

A thought came to Amanda. *Hydrophobia.* Her science teacher had said that was the other term for rabies. An infected animal could be very thirsty, yet terrified of water.

The boar rushed straight toward the cabin. It seemed to be running blind, interested only in escape, until it tripped and fell nearby. The boar struggled to its feet and saw them.

"Amanda, it's gonna charge."

There was no time to flee. She looked desperately for a weapon. Propped up against the wall of the cabin was an old rusty shovel. Amanda grabbed the handle and raised the tool like a club over her head.

7

The boar came a few steps closer, shaking its head back and forth. Those murderous tusks raked the air. She raised the shovel high over her head and swung. The metal scoop struck the boar's head and broke from the handle. With a shriek of pain the animal retreated.

Still holding the broken handle, Amanda gripped Jordan's arm.

"Now, inside!" She half-shoved and dragged him into the cabin.

Jordan collapsed to the floor. Amanda tossed the handle aside and slammed the door. Panting, she leaned against the wood. Outside it was quiet again. Through the window she saw that the boar had struggled to its feet. The shovel had opened a gash on the animal's forehead and now the boar stared with one good eye at the cabin. Amanda was convinced the beast was glaring at her.

"That's right," she said. "If you know what's good for you, you'll stay clear of us." Even though she was scared, she knew she had hurt the boar. She felt braver.

A moan startled her. Jordan sat up, looking dazed. "Who are you talking to?"

"The pig." She stepped toward him. "Let me check that bandage."

The wrapping had come loose so she retied it. More blood had seeped through.

"Can I get up?" he asked. "This floor's pretty hard."

"Are you sure?"

"Um, yeah. Maybe in the chair."

The one chair in the cabin, maybe a hundred years old, was the putrid green color of dried vomit. The cushion had a gaping hole, with stuffing spilling out like shaving cream. She swept the stuffing aside and tried to ignore the sprinklings of mouse droppings. Was the mouse still burrowed inside the cushion? How, she wondered, could anyone live like this?

She helped Jordan into the chair. He panted from the effort, then looked around.

"Nice place," he said.

"Yeah, maybe you'll want to move here, instead of Edmonton?"

In one corner was a wood stove, the kind that had hot plates on top for cooking. A gouged wooden table and chairs and a single bed with a faded blue blanket and rumpled pillow completed the furnishings. Near the stove was a cupboard and counter top. When she opened a cupboard door something inside moved. She hoped it was nothing more than a mouse.

Amanda found a bag of chips that had been gnawed through, with crumbs scattered around. A plastic peanut butter jar, also chewed open, contents smeared across the shelf. A box of wooden matches. The matches seemed dry, so she put them in her pocket. Who knew how long they would be trapped here?

She checked the rest of the cupboard and found some chipped plates and a filthy coffee cup. On her hands and knees she peered into the furthest corner. At the very back was a can. She reached for it.

"Hey, cola!"

Jordan smiled weakly. "I'll drink mine out of the can."

The top of the can was dirty, including some black little pellets that looked suspiciously like mouse droppings. Amanda shook them into a corner and wiped the top of the can with her shirt.

Popping the tab, she handed it over to Jordan. "Sorry about the dirt. The health inspectors wouldn't like this."

Jordan grabbed the drink and took several big gulps. "Mmm, really good stuff. Nicely aged." Then he smiled and passed the cola back to her.

The thought of the grime on the can made her pause. But she was really thirsty. "Thanks."

She swallowed the last of the drink. It was pretty awful, warm and too sweet, but wet. Funny how things change: a few hours earlier, all she could think about was getting online with her chat buddy Tara from Saskatoon.

"I'm still thirsty." Jordan leaned his head back to rest on the chair.

She reached out and touched him. His forehead was sweaty and too warm. He looked feverish.

As if Jordan could read her thoughts, he asked, "Do you think I'm getting rabies?"

"No. Of course not. It takes a lot longer to show up."

"Then why do I feel so lousy?"

Blood loss. Shock, she thought. What does a person do for that? Amanda leaned down and put her arm around his shoulder. "I don't know. We'll get you out of here and to a hospital."

He nodded and licked his lips.

Seeing him so weak made her realize she had no choice. "Jordan, I'm going to try to get Nick's truck and bring it back in front of the cabin."

Alarmed, Jordan shook his head. "The boar."

She looked at his leg. A trickle of blood had run down his thigh to drip onto the floor. They needed to get out as soon as possible.

"I can outrun it, I think."

She opened the door carefully and peered outside. The boar wasn't in the yard. Or in the garden. Maybe the animal had wandered into the woods. Or drowned in the river. Nope, that would be too easy.

"Be right back."

She stepped outside and gently closed the door. One of the boards on the tiny porch creaked. She froze, but nothing changed. No deadly tusks, no huge hairy body. She leaped from the porch and ran.

Reaching the farmer's body, Amanda fought an impulse to retreat. She kept her gaze averted and carefully stepped around Nick to look in the truck. Her heart sank. There was no key in the ignition. Nothing on the seat or the floor, either.

Maybe he still had the keys in a pocket. She hated the idea of touching a dead person. But there was no other way. Dropping to her knees, she checked his pockets only to find a few coins and some cigarettes. He must have dropped the keys somewhere.

Amanda scrambled along the ground, searching beside the truck and even under it. She leaned against the truck, trying to think. Where had the boar attacked him? She turned and saw the pig pen with the gate wide open.

Amanda headed for the pen, studying the ground. Nick's path was marked by blotches of drying blood that appeared every few feet in the grass. When she reached the pen, she moaned in disappointment. The inside of the pen was a mass of dirt, mud and manure. It would be almost impossible to find anything there.

She walked toward the cabin, fighting back tears. When Amanda was near the quad she remembered a chocolate bar stored in the compartment. She headed for the disabled vehicle.

8

The boar lay on his side in the shade of the quad. His breath came in shallow puffs that made his massive ribs rise and fall. His head hurt, badly. After that girl had hit him with the shovel, his brain seemed ready to split open. His left eye was completely closed and covered in blood. A fly walked across the wound and down to his nostril.

The sound of the cabin door opening and closing had caught his attention. He raised his head and the pain in his skull radiated like an exploding sun. His head sank again against the flattened tire. He had killed this beast and now its body gave him some protection from the intense light.

Suddenly another shadow fell across the ground beside him. His good eye saw the girl. She paused beside the quad, looking behind and beside her, all around except where he lay. She reached for the machine, looking for something. Smiled as she took out a bag and then looked down. At him.

She gasped. The seat lid of the quad slipped from her fingers and landed with a bang. The noise was a bright needle piercing his ear and entering his brain. The boar groaned and grunted. He rolled to his side and tried to get up.

The girl jerked a step backward. He could smell fear on her body. Suddenly she spun around and ran.

◆   ◆   ◆

Amanda raced to the cabin, opened the door and slammed it behind her.

Jordan's eyes jerked open and he began to rise from the chair. "What's …?"

She peeked through the window. The boar stood just in front of the quad. It had made no move to come after her.

"The beast," she said. "It was resting beside the quad."

"What's it doing now?"

"Nothing. It looks almost dead."

"Good." Jordan breathed deeply. "What have you got there?"

She had forgotten the chocolate bar. "A treat." She ripped open the chocolate, broke off a chunk and handed the rest to him.

"Mmm," Jordan grinned. "Best meal I've ever had."

Jordan looked at his leg. Dried blood covered his thigh and calf and stained his shoe.

"What time do you think it is?"

Shadows from trees behind the cabin had stretched out to the quad. Amanda shrugged. "Don't know. Must be after supper, though."

"People will be wondering where we are. They'll come looking."

A sudden thought hit her. "Does anybody actually know where we are?"

The look on his face alarmed her. He avoided her gaze and stared at the floor.

"Well...."

"You didn't tell anybody, did you?"

"How could I? We were just out, you know, riding."

Right: one more hill, one more drink. "Maybe it wouldn't hurt, once in a while, to plan things out. If you know what you're going to do before, then stuff doesn't happen."

"Oh, so now this is my fault." He crumpled the empty candy wrapper and threw it aside. "Sure, I knew there was a crazy pig out here. I knew the quad would have problems. That's why I took it. I knew it would be more fun this way."

"No. No, it's not your fault. I'm sorry, I just...."

Amanda crossed the floor and put her hand on his shoulder. Angrily, he shrugged it off.

"People might be looking for us, Jordan. The later it gets, the more likely they'll come."

She didn't put into words what worried her most. How would anyone know where to look? The forest lands were deep, stretching for hundreds of miles.

"Yeah," he said. "They'll come."

Jordan shifted in the chair and winced. Blood seeped through the bandage.

She pulled one of the kitchen chairs over and lifted his injured leg onto it. "We should elevate this."

His face was pale and his eyes red. "Amanda, I'm thinking that you should just go. Try to make it over the bridge. Water scares the pig, you said. It won't follow you. Then, you could find your way back to the main road."

"Not by myself. I'm not leaving you here alone."

"I'll be fine. You said yourself nobody knows where we are. It could take a long for help to get here."

She glanced outside. The shadows had covered the cabin and now stretched as far as the river. The boar was nowhere in sight.

Then, faintly, she noticed something. "Did you hear that?"

"What?"

She opened the door a crack. There was the sound again. Not the higher pitch of a quad or motorcycle. "An engine. A truck maybe."

"I hear it too. Can you see anything?"

"No."

Abruptly the sound stopped. Then Amanda hear a door slam shut. She strained, listening, but didn't hear a motor or anything else. She couldn't stand to wait any longer. Jerking the door open, Amanda yelled.

"Hello. Help! Over here!"

"See anybody?" Jordan rose painfully from his chair and hobbled over to stand beside her. He rested his arm on her shoulder.

"Not yet," she said.

She called out again, then waited. Minutes flowed by like the water under the bridge. She yelled several more times. Finally, Amanda saw movement where the dirt path disappeared in the trees. A man walked slowly down the track toward the bridge. He stopped to shield his eyes against the setting sun. "Hello?"

9

Amanda cupped her hands to her mouth and shouted. "Can you help us?"

The man reached into a pocket and raised binoculars to his eyes. He lowered them again. "What's the problem?"

"My boyfriend is hurt. He needs to get to a hospital."

Jordan limped past her and stood in the open to wave.

The man took a few steps closer. "What's wrong with him?"

"He's cut badly." How could she say, in a few words, that they'd been attacked by an insane pig. He might think they were crazy and leave.

The man used the binoculars again. He would be able to see Jordan's leg, the bandage and probably the blood. He called again. "What happened?"

Now she had to say it. "We were attacked by a boar."

"Good grief." The man shielded his eyes again, scanning the area. "Is it still around?"

"I think so."

"Okay. Stay put. I'll be right back."

Amanda leaned against the door frame, sighing with relief.

The man slipped from view and was gone for several minutes. When he reappeared, he held something as he crossed to the river.

"What's he carrying?" Amanda wondered aloud.

"Looks like a gun." Jordan teetered and leaned heavily against her.

They watched the stranger as he slowly crossed the bridge. He looked at the broken timber and then at the wrecked quad. His eyes roamed the area, pausing often to check out the two young people. He wore jeans, a camouflage shirt and a dark green cap with the words Sure Shot on it. When he drew near, he stepped onto the porch and stared at Jordan's leg.

"That's the oddest bear wound I've ever seen."

"Not a bear," Amanda said. "Boar. You know, a large pig."

He blinked. "A boar. You sure?"

"Believe me, we both got a good look at it. And, it attacked the farmer who lived here. He's dead."

"Dead?" His face showed disbelief.

She shuddered at the memory of Nick's lifeless body. "You can look if you want. Over there."

The hunter could see Nick's crumpled body across the yard. He took a step as if to check for himself. Then his face paled and he looked away.

"A wild boar did all this?" He shook his head.

"The tusks are this long." Amanda held her hands apart. "Razor sharp. The boar is sick, too, drooling and acting strange. Like it has rabies."

"A boar," the man said. "I've never hunted one of them before." He blinked, as if remembering something. He held out his hand. "Name is Bailey. George Bailey."

Amanda shook his hand and asked, "Do you have a phone? Ours is broken."

"Back in the truck. I'll call, but your friend needs some attention right away."

He propped his rifle against the cabin and dropped to one knee beside Jordan. "That's a bad cut. How long ago?"

Amanda told him and he frowned. "We have to stop the bleeding. He needs stitches."

All the moving around had worked the bandage loose. Fresh, shiny blood trickled down Jordan's leg.

"I've got a first-aid kit in my truck. After I make the call, we'll fix the bandage, then move you out. I'll be right back."

"Shouldn't we just take him to the truck and do it there?"

George shook his head and lowered his voice. "Your friend is looking pretty weak. If he loses any more blood, he could go into shock." He patted her arm. "This won't take long. I'll be right back."

She started to protest, but he grabbed the rifle and gave Amanda a reassuring smile before leaving. Back inside, Amanda watched him through the window as he hurried across the yard to the bridge. He studied the woods and garden as he went. The boar was nowhere in sight as the hunter crossed the river and disappeared into the woods.

Long minutes passed. Amanda stayed at the window, anxious, wondering. What if he didn't come back? What if he decided that two kids out in the bush weren't his problem?

As if he read her thoughts, Jordan suddenly spoke. "Maybe he changed his mind."

Amanda spun around to face him. "Don't be silly. He's not going to just abandon us. He had to make the call first."

Jordan shrugged and she went back to watching at the window. How far was the truck? Amanda remembered how she had felt when they first saw the hunter coming. The gun had relieved her, but also stirred a twinge of uneasiness. Serial killers picked out strangers, innocent people, to murder. She had heard too many news stories and watched too many horror movies.

"Amanda." Jordan held his hand out. "This is a mess. My fault."

"Never mind that now." She leaned over and kissed his forehead, which was warm and sticky.

"I wonder," he said.

"What?"

"If angels are as pretty as you."

She laughed. "You're delirious."

"Yeah. Sure am." He grinned and for a moment there was that mischievous smile that made her feel all funny inside.

A sound outdoors caught her attention. "Hold that thought." Jumping up, she rushed to the window.

Nothing. Just woods, river and sky. Then, a flash of movement in the trees on the path. George's truck came down the dirt track and stopped on the other side of the river.

"There he is!" Amanda turned to Jordan. "See, told you!"

She opened the door to watch the hunter as he got out and started to cross the river. He had his rifle slung over his shoulder and carried a red box. Relief swept over her. He picked his way carefully over the planks.

When he saw her, he waved. "Rescue people are on their way."

Amanda grinned widely and said to Jordan, "He made the call, and help is coming."

She looked back to see the hunter step from the near end of the bridge. A clump of bush beside him trembled, as if it had been shaken. Suddenly the boar burst through it.

Amanda yelled, "Look out!"

The hunter froze. In the split second that it took for him to turn, the boar lunged. The animal hit him in the legs and Bailey fell on his back onto the bridge. The rifle jerked from his shoulder and clattered to the boards.

As the hunter tried to stand the boar attacked him again, swinging its tusks. Scuttling backwards, the hunter grabbed the rifle and began to raise it just as the boar rammed him once more.

The rifle flew end over end into the river. Horrified, Amanda threw the door open and hit the ground running. She didn't know what she was going to do, just that her rescuer needed help. As she ran, the boar drove his head into George's chest. The hunter screamed as the boar hooked and raised him from the planks. Then it tossed him over the side and into the water.

Amanda stumbled and fell. From the ground, she could see Bailey claw at the sides of the bank, struggling against the current. Frantic, she looked down and saw a pile of rocks picked from the garden. She stooped for the nearest stones and started throwing them at the boar.

"Die, you stupid pig. Go away!"

She hurled one rock the size of a soft ball. It soared straight to its mark and hit the boar. Startled, the animal squealed and looked her way. With a grunt that ended in a roar, it churned up the bank and rushed at her.

Empty-handed, Amanda turned and ran.

10

She made it to the cabin, dove inside and slammed the door. No sooner had the door closed when the boar smashed into it. ***BOOM!*** Boards cracked.

Jordan struggled to his feet. "Come on," he yelled. "Help me with the chair."

They shoved the chair up against the door. There was another thunderous impact and the latch loosened as the doorframe splintered.

"It's coming in!" Jordan threw himself against the chair.

But nothing happened. The only sound from the other side of the door was a labored breathing. A wet sound, gross.

Amanda tiptoed to the window. The boar stood several feet from the cabin. Its damaged eye was now completely closed and its mouth was all bloody. The animal weaved from side to side, as if trying to decide what to do. Then it suddenly turned and stumbled a short distance away.

She saw the hunter in the water. His hand raised once, as if in a final appeal to her. Then, slowly, his body slipped all the way into the current. He rolled once, face down. The swift river carried him away.

"No. Oh please, no."

Amanda slumped against the wall and sobbed. Before today, she had never seen anyone die. Now there was death all around and especially outside, waiting. She wanted it all to go away. *Please*, she prayed. *Let it stop.*

Jordan touched her arm. "The hunter?"

She shook her head. "Gone, in the river. I think he's dead."

Jordan put his hands over his face. He looked defeated and afraid, she thought, the way she felt. Suddenly another sound caught Amanda's attention. It was rhythmic, something turning slowly like an old fan.

"What's that?" She got to her feet and wiped away the tears.

A glance out the window gave her the answer. The boar stood a short distance away, rubbing its wounded face against the dirt. As it pushed its head against the ground, the boar made a low grunting sound.

"It's acting crazy," Amanda whispered.

The boar stopped, tilted its head back and let out a squeal like a human wail. Then it spun around, as if it had heard something. Finally the boar looked up, right at Amanda.

"It's coming again," she warned Jordan. As she spoke, the boar lowered its head and rushed at the cabin door.

A loud thud, and the chair moved. Another blow, and the latch flew from the doorframe.

Light flooded in through the opening. Jordan desperately tried to hold the door frame while Amanda pushed against the door itself. It was no use. Another blow knocked them from the chair to the floor. The boar's next thrust against the door would shove it open. Amanda scrambled backwards, crablike, against the far wall.

Wham! The chair tumbled aside and the door flew open. The pig shoved its head and shoulders inside the cabin. It swung its head, checking the interior. The pig's one good eye stopped when it saw Amanda.

For a moment the only sound in the cabin was the wet, raspy breathing of the boar.

Amanda had her back against the wall, hands stretched out. Her fingers touched something wooden and she glanced down. The broken shovel handle. It was better than nothing. She grasped the handle and pointed it toward the boar. A piece of stick, up against a pig the size of a bear. She fought back a whimper.

The boar grunted and lunged, its hooves tearing into the wooden floor. Desperately, Amanda pointed the broken handle at her attacker.

The boar's jaw gaped open when it reached her and the sharp end of the handle entered his mouth. She felt the shaft drive back until it jammed against the wall. Still the weight of the boar's body carried it forward until it collided with Amanda and she fell. The animal made a wet gagging sound and collapsed onto its side. In a death spasm, the boar quivered and its legs kicked, thrashing against the floorboards.

Suddenly, the boar was still. It had landed on Amanda's legs, pinning her. She felt pain in her right leg and cried out as she moved. Squirming and twisting, she pulled herself from under the beast.

The shovel handle was buried through the mouth and inside the pig like a spear. The pointed end had come out of its body near the spine. There was blood everywhere and a nasty stench filled the cabin.

"Amanda! Are you okay?" Jordan was on his hands and knees.

Pain spread through her ankle and she gasped. "I ... I don't know." She crawled over to him and they hugged.

Next to them lay the enormous body of the boar.

"It's dead!" Amanda breathed. She almost believed that the animal's corpse would get up again, like some evil creature in a terrifying movie.

Jordan managed to speak. "Huge." The animal seemed to fill the cramped space of the cabin.

Jordan crawled away from the dead boar. "Let's get out of here," he said.

Amanda helped him up and they shuffled outdoors. Jordan wanted to be as far from the cabin as possible, but when he tried to move he slumped against the steps. His head rolled to one side.

"Jordan ... Jordan!"

Amanda gently rubbed his face to wake him up. He was breathing, but unconscious. She propped him against the cabin wall and sat beside him. Minutes passed, then a half-hour. She was exhausted and, with her shoulder beside his, she dozed.

Her body jerked awake. What was that? A metallic sound, a clank. From the bridge. A truck with a rack of flashing lights on its roof was on the other side of the water. Someone had opened the gate and now the truck crept across.

Epilogue

6 weeks later

Amanda dragged and resized the two windows on her computer screen. On the left was her school report called "Survival Tips for the Outdoors." She nodded to herself. This section was about encounters with dangerous animals. She knew something about that, for sure.

The window on the right showed the Messenger box, with a list of her friends. She was talking to Tara, who had just broken up with her boyfriend. Amanda tried to be understanding, but Tara was always starting or ending a relationship. Amanda thought her friend might as well be shopping for new shoes.

The list of people "not online" included Jordan. He had moved with his father to Edmonton soon after the incident with the boar. So far, they had kept in touch, like he promised. But one thing hadn't changed about him. Jordan had his own sense of time. He might show up online when he promised or he might not. Or he did, but much later than he said.

BUZZ!

The messenger window popped up and there was Jordan's avatar, a laughing coyote. "JJ Coyote is typing" the message bar said. Then a single word appeared on the screen.

JJ: "Hi"

Amanda hesitated. The last few times they met online Jordan sounded low. Since the move to the city his mood was darker, quieter.

She typed. "Hi. What's up?"

JJ: "Tyler just left." Tyler was one of Jordan's new friends in Edmonton.

Amanda: "Oh, what's he doing?"

JJ: "Not much. He's having some people over for a party tonight. I'll probably go."

Amanda's fingers hovered over the keys without moving. There were a lot of parties in Jordan's life these days.

JJ: "Hello?"

Amanda: "I guess you didn't hear the news."

JJ: "What news?"

Amanda: "The hunter. His body was found in the river, about a day's walk from the cabin."

This time it was his turn to take a long pause. Then Jordan's cam sprang open onscreen. There he was, his usual smiling face looking flat. She activated her own video. His voice came over the speaker.

"I feel so bad about that guy."

"Yeah." Another long pause.

This was a mistake, she thought. He's already feeling low. Why did I mention the hunter? Stupid. She quickly changed the subject.

"How are you doing?"

After the boar attack, Jordan's leg had healed slowly. His doctor said Jordan had muscle damage in the leg. It could be something he would have to accept for the rest of his life. He walked with a limp now.

"Okay, I guess." His voice was flat, listless. Lately the happy, joking person she had fallen in love with was missing. He often sounded depressed. Sometimes she was afraid for him.

Jordan was tapping on the desk with a pencil. *Tick, tick.* His hair covered one eye and the other avoided looking into the cam at her. When he spoke again, his voice was low, soft.

"I get so lonely here, Amanda," he said. "This city is big and people are always in a hurry. It's like everybody is a stranger. I miss life in town. I miss you."

Maybe it was the right time to share her idea with him. "I've been thinking."

"Oh oh, trouble ahead when Amanda's brain is working." There was a flash of the old smile, the teasing.

"Funny. Are you going to let me talk?"

"Sure." His screen image leaned back in the chair, hands behind his head.

She took a deep breath, not sure how this would go. "You remember how I said my dad's business is getting really busy?" Her father ran a gas station and repair shop. Lately, he was so busy with work he was putting in very long days.

When Jordan didn't comment, she continued. "Well, he needs help. Last night he said he wished you were still here. He'd offer you a job."

"Really?" Jordan's eyes widened.

"He knows you like to work on engines. He said he could teach you the other stuff."

Jordan shook his head. "I don't know if I can work. My leg, you know."

She knew. She also knew that he was starting to use it as an excuse. He rarely went outdoors, spending most of his time in his room.

"You might have to move more slowly, but you can still do almost everything like before."

"Um. Well, anyway, I'm not there."

"You could stay with your aunt."

Jordan shook his head. "My uncle wouldn't want me there."

"He won't have much to say about it."

"What do you mean?"

"Your aunt went to the police after one of their fights. He broke her cheekbone. He's moved out and he's not allowed near the house."

"No way."

"Yeah. And I think she's lonely. You'd be company for her."

Now Jordan rested his head on his hands and stared into the screen at her. "Your dad would actually hire me?"

"Yes. He says you'd make a good worker."

Jordan took a deep breath. "I want to be with you. And, I guess I'm homesick. Do you really think people want me back there?"

"You know I do." Amanda smiled.

He reached for something in front of him and held up a phone. "I'm going to call my aunt now, see if it's okay to stay with her." He began punching the numbers. "Oh, and Amanda?"

"Yes?"

"The next time we go out on a quad, you have to promise me something."

The simple mention of the quad made her stomach do a roll. She would think twice before getting back on one of those machines. Her voice was cautious. "What?"

"You have to promise you won't try to talk me into going on a pig hunt."

She laughed. "Deal."

Suddenly he held up a finger to Amanda: *wait.* "Hey, auntie Teena, guess who? Yeah, it's me, your favorite nephew."

He began nodding and the biggest grin she had seen on Jordan's face in a long time spread over his features. "I know, I know. Yeah, I really miss seeing you too."

Jordan reached for the keyboard as he spoke. A message popped up on her screen.

The message was only four letters long:

ttyl

And then another message, even shorter, but better:

sys

978-0-595-47855-2
0-595-47855-7

Printed in the United States
135497LV00001B/11/P